Cocurricular Activities:
Their Values and Benefits

Academic Societies and Competitions
Striving for Excellence

Career Preparation Clubs
Goal Oriented

Community Service
Lending a Hand

Foreign Language Clubs
Discovering Other Cultures

Hobby Clubs
Sharing Your Interests

Intramural Sports
Joining the Team

School Publications
Adventures in Media

Science and Technology Clubs
Ideas and Inventions

Student Government and Class Activities
Leaders of Tomorrow

Theater, Speech, and Dance
Expressing Your Talents

Vocal and Instrumental Groups
Making Music

Foreign Language Clubs
Discovering Other Cultures

Betty Bolté

Mason Crest Publishers
Philadelphia

Mason Crest Publishers, Inc.
370 Reed Road
Broomall, PA 19008
(866) MCP-BOOK (toll free)
www.masoncrest.com

First printing

1 2 3 4 5 6 7 8 9 10

Library of Congress Cataloging-in-Publication Data

Bolte, Betty.
   Foreign language clubs: discovering other cultures/by Betty Bolte.
      p. cm.— (Cocurricular activities)
   ISBN 1-59084-894-2
1. Languages, Modern—Study and teaching (Secondary) 2. Intercultural communication. I. Title. II. Series. PB36.B63 2005
   418'.0071'2—dc22
      2004015862

Produced by
Choptank Syndicate, Inc. and Chestnut Productions, L.L.C.
260 Upper Moss Hill Road
Russell, Massachusetts 01071

Project Editors Norman Macht and Mary Hull
Design and Production Lisa Hochstein
Picture Research Mary Hull

OPPOSITE TITLE PAGE

The Eiffel Tower, illuminated at night, soars over the city of Paris. Joining a language club is a great way to explore another country, immerse yourself in the culture, and perhaps have the opportunity to travel abroad.

Table of Contents

Introduction

COCURRICULAR ACTIVITIES BUILD CHARACTER

Sharon L. Ransom
Chief Officer of the Office of Standards-Based Instruction
for Chicago Public Schools

Cocurricular activities provide an assortment of athletic, musical, cultural, dramatic, club, and service activities. They provide opportunities based on different talents and interests for students to find their niche while developing character. Character is who we really are. It's what we say and how we say it, what we think, what we value, and how we conduct ourselves in difficult situations. It is character that often determines our success in life and cocurricular activities play a significant role in the development of character in young men and women.

Cocurricular programs and activities provide opportunities to channel the interests and talents of students into positive efforts for the betterment of themselves and the community as a whole. Students who participate in cocurricular activities are often expected to follow certain rules and regulations that prepare them for challenges as well as opportunities later in life.

Many qualities that build character are often taught and nurtured through participation in cocurricular activities. A student learns to make commitments and stick with them through victories and losses as well as achievements and disappointments. They can also learn to build relationships and work collaboratively with others, set goals, and follow the principles and rules of the discipline, club, activity, or sport in which they participate.

Students who are active in cocurricular activities are often successful in school because the traits and behaviors they learn outside of the classroom are important in acquiring and maintaining their academic success. Students become committed to their studies and set academic goals that lead them to triumph. When they relate behaviors, such as following rules or directions or teaming with others, to the classroom, this can result in improved academic achievement.

Students who participate in cocurricular activities and acquire these character-rich behaviors and traits are not likely to be involved in negative behaviors. Peer pressure and negative influences are not as strong for these students, and they are not likely to be involved with drugs, alcohol, or tobacco use. They also attend school more regularly and are less likely to drop out of school.

Students involved in cocurricular activities often are coached or mentored by successful and ethical adults of good and strong character who serve as role models and assist students in setting their goals for the future. These students are also more likely to graduate from high school and go on to college because of their involvement in co-curricular activities.

In this series you will come to realize the many benefits of cocurricular activities. These activities bring success and benefits to individual students, the school, and the community.

A riverside hotel situated in the Bavarian countryside. Many language students have the desire to travel to a foreign country. Joining a language club and working to raise funds are two ways to work toward this goal.

1

Experiencing a New Culture

"**G**uten tag! Willkommen zum Deutschklub!" Susan Miller greets each student as they arrive for their monthly German Club meeting. At South Carroll High School, located west of Sykesville, Maryland, the language clubs, as well as all other school clubs, meet on Activity Day once a month.

As the German Club advisor for the past eight years, Ms. Miller knows how to make the most of the thirty minutes each month. She recognizes that the opportunity to have the clubs meet during school hours makes it possible for every student to participate in a cocurricular activity. That means more of her German students, current and past, can also share in learning about the German culture and language. Ms. Miller makes sure that some form of cultural and language activity occurs at each meeting. Often she has help in making that happen.

The students, as well as the German exchange students the school hosts, gather to enjoy and experience a wide variety of games and activities. A German friend, Sigrid Rodgers, helps Ms. Miller each month with the activities. The club officers plan vocabulary games to broaden the club's German word bank. The club also plays Pictionary and charades, answers trivia questions, and matches

Facts About Foreign Language Study

Who studies foreign languages in the United States?

- Over 4 million elementary school students
- Over 3 million junior high school/middle school students
- Over 7 million high school students
- 51 percent of all public high school students
- 78 percent of all private high school students

Among secondary schools in the United States that offer foreign language programs:

- 93 percent offer Spanish
- 64 percent offer French
- 24 percent offer German
- 20 percent offer Latin
- 7 percent offer Japanese
- 3 percent offer Italian or Russian
- 2 percent offer American Sign Language or Hebrew
- 1 percent offer Chinese or Greek

Source: *A National Study of Foreign Language Instruction in Elementary and Secondary Schools, 1998,* funded by the U.S. Department of Education and conducted by Lucinda Branaman and Nancy Rhodes of the Center for Applied Linguistics.

German club events at South Carroll High in Sykesville, Maryland,
include a Frühlingsfest celebration in which students receive instruction
in traditional German dance.

German and English words in a bilingual matching game.
They learn about holidays and traditions. Foreign exchange
students attending the school are asked to share their
personal experiences. One Christmas the students made
German desserts to share, such as Apfelkuchen (apple cake),
Deutscher Scholadenkuchen (German chocolate cake), and
many kinds of cookies.

The students look forward to eating rich food, but also
the chance to play games, sing songs and Christmas carols
like "Die Schnitzelbank," and learn traditional dances. A
local German couple, Mr. and Mrs. Richard Skowronek,
bring their German dance group to the school to share
dances with the club members. Members who may be
reluctant to hit the dance floor are soon up and dancing to
the energetic music.

Sigrid Rodgers also invites students from the German
club to her home during the summer for a German picnic.
Imagine standing outside on a lovely summer day, chomp-
ing down on sausages, potato salad, and schnitzel while

listening to German music and watching traditional German dancing.

The German Club also travels to nearby McDaniels College in Westminster, Maryland, where professor of German Dr. Mohamed Esa has sponsored an annual German-American Day for the past nine years. Workshops at the event include German Dancing, Cheese Making, and Careers Using German, as well as a lecture entitled

Popular Foreign Languages

According to a 2002 Modern Language Association survey, more American students are studying foreign languages than ever before, and the variety of those languages is greater now than at any time since 1958, when the first Modern Language Association survey was released. The fifteen most studied foreign languages are, in order:

1. Spanish
2. French
3. German
4. Italian
5. American Sign Language
6. Japanese
7. Chinese
8. Latin
9. Russian
10. Ancient Greek
11. Biblical Hebrew
12. Arabic
13. Modern Hebrew
14. Portuguese
15. Korean

"Surviving the Holocaust." A music program is presented to the nine hundred German students and their teachers. Everyone enjoys a traditional German lunch consisting of sausages, potato pancakes, applesauce, and German desserts, as well as American pizza. Each year, a student from one of the local high schools designs a T-shirt for the event that the college then prints up and distributes to each student who attends.

The South Carroll High School German Club has existed for 30 years, with about 25 members per year. Some of those students have gone on to study German at college, or apply for an exchange program scholarship.

The German Club hosted an annual Spring Festival—a Frühlingsfest—from 1991 to 2000 in the evening at the school cafeteria. Parents, the school community, and

A Musical Introduction to Germany

What better way to learn about a country than to study its arts and culture? The Indianapolis Symphony Orchestra (ISO) has created a way to enhance the high school foreign language curriculum by providing the opportunity to understand another culture through great works of music.

The ISO offers local high school German clubs the chance to expand their knowledge of German culture through a special "German night" at the symphony, which features the greatest composers and music of the country. The concert begins with an introductory speech, followed by an exciting array of music from composers like Beethoven and Wagner. A special post-concert reception is then held, giving the language students and their teachers a chance to meet the musicians.

If you live near a city orchestra, why not check with them to see if they are interested in starting a similar program for your country of interest?

For high school students studying German, the American Association of Teachers of German sponsors group travel to Germany. Students travel in a small group with an American teacher of German as chaperone. They spend three weeks attending classes at a high school, living with a German host family, and participating in excursions to places of cultural and historic significance.

other county German classes were invited. Mr. and Mrs. Skowronek brought their traditional German dancers in native costumes to entertain. The club charged a modest admission fee of $2.00, which was then given to the dance group. Additionally, German musicians played for the attendees. Students performed for the audience by reading, dancing, and singing. Delicious German desserts were served and savored.

Each year, the German club paints a cafeteria window at the high school to celebrate the Homecoming activities, and they help create a float for the Homecoming parade. In

2003, the German, French, and Spanish clubs joined forces to prepare a float.

Being a member of an active club helps each member feel like part of something bigger and better than just attending classes at school. They experience a taste of another culture and make new friends.

Studying the history, art, and architecture of a country can make a travel experience that much more rewarding. In language clubs, members have the opportunity to look at a culture in depth.

2

Getting to Know Language Clubs

What language clubs does your school offer? Most middle and high schools have a foreign language in their curriculum, but not all have language clubs associated with them. The most commonly taught foreign languages are Spanish, French, German, and Latin. That doesn't mean you won't find Japanese or Russian, or maybe even Greek. Sometimes Latin and Greek are combined into an International or Classics Club. Whatever language you're studying can be the basis for a club.

Clubs of all kinds exist so that people who share a common interest can get together and learn about it while making new friends and meeting with old ones. Through a club, you will learn more about another culture, which makes it easier for you to accept differences between yourself and others. By studying a different language and culture you will further your understanding of people around the world who have the same basic needs, but different ways of meeting them.

In language clubs, students meet on a regular basis to talk in the chosen language. Meeting times depend on the schedule at your school, the desires of the club members, and the teacher's availability. Meetings happen once a month, once a week, or as needed, for anywhere from thirty minutes to an hour or more. During the meetings, you might play games, sing songs, write a letter or story, or draw as you learn more about the culture of the language you have chosen.

In the process of meeting each month, club members learn about each other as well as the language. Soon friendships form. The club advisor is normally a teacher. Teachers enjoy a chance to relate to students on a more individual level, sharing a common interest rather than a forced curriculum.

The club has the ability to connect with both state and national organizations that can provide support and opportunities that are broader than what a typical school can offer. For example, state foreign language organizations, such as the Alabama Federation of French Clubs, offer state language tests, with prizes that include scholarship money for college.

Membership in a language club allows you to see life from a different perspective. You'll notice a different structure to the language. You'll likely enjoy different foods, different customs and traditions. Yet, through looking at the differences, you'll also find the similarities. If you look for them, you'll find that though the language is different, it still allows people to talk, to laugh, to share their day's events. And though the music may include some different instruments, like castanets or tubas, you'll find that it still makes people tap their toes and smile.

Being in a language club also helps you make friends

There are many ways to learn about your country of study—from practicing the language, watching foreign films, listening to music, to experiencing the foods people living there enjoy.

because you have something in common. You have a safe place where you can get to know other students in your school and decide if you want to make them your friends. Your friendships will include students of all ages and abilities in the language. You may find yourself helping another student who is having a hard time grasping the language. You might enjoy translating foreign music into English, or American music into another language. Most of all, though, membership means fun: trying new foods, new music, new books and art work, dances, and fables.

Language clubs also give you a chance to increase the amount of knowledge and understanding you have in your language class, by helping you use the language in natural conversations and situations.

National language organizations give national level exams that students from middle school to high school can take to win prizes as well as recognition for their school and club. Your teacher or advisor can help you prepare for any of these tests.

Each February to March, the National Spanish Examinations are given. All high school students enrolled in first through third year Spanish are eligible to take this exam. Using multiple-choice questions, the exam gives you a chance to show how well you can read and listen to Spanish. More information on the test can be found at the NSE Web site. First through fifth place scores at the national level receive a plaque. Additional prizes are possible from local American Association of Teachers of Spanish and Portuguese (AATSP) chapters.

The National German Test, sponsored by the American Association of Teachers of German (AATG), is available to all second through fourth level high school German students. The highest scoring seniors are awarded a four-week study trip to Germany, where they stay with a German host family and tour different regions of the country. Other scholarships are also available. Check their Web site for specific details.

If you like French, perhaps you'd like to try to win a scholarship to the American University in Paris. You can enter Le Grand Concours French Test, just like 95,530 students in first through sixth grades did in 2003. Prizes include Olympic gold, silver, and bronze medals as well as other cool awards.

The National Junior Classical League (NJCL) offers many activities for people who enjoy studying ancient Greek and Latin culture, literature, and language. The NJCL helps others understand how important Greek and Latin are to our own culture. Once you graduate from high school, you can join the National Senior Classical League to continue

National Language Organizations

The American Classical League
Miami University
422 Wells Mill Drive, Oxford, OH 45056
ph: (513) 529-7741
email: info@aclclassics.org
www.aclclassics.org

National Latin Exam
Mary Washington College
1301 College Avenue, Fredericksburg, VA 22401
email: nle@mwc.edu
www.nle.org

Excellence Through Classics
National Mythology Exam
www.etclassics.org

Medusa Mythology Examination
P.O. Box 1032, Gainesville, VA 20156
ph: (800) 896-4671
email: info@medusaexam.org
www.medusaexam.org

National Spanish Examination,
2051 Mt. Zion Drive, Golden, CO 80401-1737
ph: (303) 278-1021
email: martha.quiat@mho.ne
www.2nse.org

National German Examination
American Association of Teachers of German
112 Haddontowne Ct., #104, Cherry Hill, NJ 08034-3668
ph: (856) 795-5553
email: headquarters@aatg.org
www.aatg.org/programs

Le Grand Concours AATF National French Contest
AATF National Headquarters
Mailcode 4510
Southern Illinois University, Carbondale, IL 62901-4510
ph: (618) 453-5731
email: abrate@siu.edu
www.frenchteachers.org/concours

Exploring the food of another country is a fun way to learn about that country's culture and history.

your involvement and study of the classics, as well as help the league with their activities.

The American Classical League (ACL) and the National Junior Classical League (NJCL) offer the National Greek Exam each year to high school students taking first, second, or third year Attic or Homeric Greek. The Beginning Attic exam is for high school students only. You can order copies of previous National Greek Exams to study from the ACL Web site.

The National Latin Exam is offered by the American Classical League and National Junior Classical League. This exam is taken by more than 128,000 students from many countries, including the United States, Australia, Belgium, New Zealand, the Republic of Niger, Switzerland, and Zimbabwe. Students must be enrolled in a Latin class to take the exam, which is offered at varying levels of difficulty. Interested students can order previous exams to study, or view and print them from the Web site. Awards for the high scorers range from a hand-lettered certificate for perfect papers, to a gold or silver medal to first- and second-place winners. Gold medal winners in certain categories will be given the chance to apply for a $1,000 college scholarship.

If you are interested in Latin or Greek mythology, maybe you would rather take the Medusa Mythology Examination, which all high school students are eligible to take. This exam gives talented students a chance to excel and be recognized, as well as to help as many students as possible learn more about mythology. If you are one of the highest scoring students, you could receive a certificate or medal from Italy, or perhaps even an Achievement Award to help you with future educational expenses. You can go to their Web site to look at and print past exams, as well as use their online practice tests to help you prepare to take the test.

Another mythology exam for classics lovers is the National Mythology Exam sponsored by the Excellence Through Classics organization. This test has been available for fourteen years to students in grades three through nine. Visit their Web site for more details on what is tested and how to prepare.

Joining a language club is usually simple. Ask your language teacher, or a friend you know who is in the club. If all else fails, the school office will direct you to the advisor for the club.

Before you make a commitment to join the club, check with your parent or guardian to be sure they approve and will allow you to attend.

To join the club you need a few things:

- An interest in learning more about the language and culture.

- Usually, to be a student (past or present) of the club's language—French for French club, German for German club, etc.
- A way to attend the meetings. If the club meets during school hours, that's easy. If it meets after school, you'll need to make sure you have a safe way to be there for the meetings and a way home.
- Be aware of any additional criteria your school may have for participating in cocurricular activities (grades, attendance, etc.).

Once you decide you want to be part of the language club, you will probably wonder, "Now what?" How will you fit in? What's expected of you?

To get the most from your club membership, try to participate in the activities offered. Remember, you're there to have fun, make friends, and experience the culture and language. You can only do that by being involved.

Make it a point to give of your talents as well as your experience. If you love to draw or paint, offer to help design and decorate projects as they arise. If you love to research, perhaps you can find out more about an upcoming holiday, festival, or other event. If you have friends at other schools, talk to them to find out about the kinds of activities their language clubs sponsor and share the new ideas with your club.

When asked to bring an item to the next meeting, be sure to do so. Most people learn best by actually doing a project, rather than merely reading about it or watching someone else do it. If you're involved in a group project, be sure to do your part. Forgetting to bring in your part of the project, or simply not doing an activity for the group's project, only leads to hard feelings from the other students in your club.

Be polite to your fellow club members and remember they have feelings, too. After all, the club is there to help every member have a better, deeper understanding of the language and culture and to make friends with others who share this interest.

You may be able to find music from your country of study at your school's language lab. Listening to and translating foreign music can be a fun way to help learn another language.

3

Activities and Events

Each language club has its own set of limits it must work within. If the club has been around for a long time, most of the routines are already set. If your club is new, you'll need to think about what your club wants to do at its meetings and for its community, if you want to take field trips, and if you want to plan a special event.

Monthly meetings of language clubs should involve some form of cultural or language activity. These activities might include any of the following:

- Charades, using the foreign language.
- Matching English with foreign language words.
- Making a traditional craft.
- Cooking or planning a traditional menu.
- Listening to and translating music.
- Playing games, such as Pictionary.
- Learning a traditional or contemporary dance.
- Becoming pen pals with a club in a different country, and writing letters sharing your life with them.

- Collecting travel brochures from a travel agent and making a collage of famous places in the country.
- Creating a video production about the culture, including photos, music, information on the history of the country, as well as what living there is like today.
- Becoming a sister club to a club in another country.
- Having refreshments at your club that are typical of those you'd find in the culture being studied.

Field trips are fun to plan. The club should decide where they want to visit—such as a restaurant, festival, or art exhibit—then discuss how they will afford to make the trip. One type of special event for a language club is an International Celebration with the other language clubs at your school. You can dress up in costumes, prepare games,

Making Your Club Great

The most important thing each club member can do to ensure an active, healthy club is to attend the meetings.

Remember, you are all there to share a common interest, a curiosity toward a language and culture. To receive the most reward from your joint efforts, it's important that everyone work together.

At your first meeting each year, suggest that everyone attending introduce themselves. Perhaps they can say something about why they are there, or if they've traveled abroad, or what their favorite color or song is. The goal is to get everyone talking and sharing.

If your advisor is leading the group, be sure you are actively listening, participating, and making suggestions. Keep in mind that this club is for all the members, and that the advisor wants to help you have a great time as you explore this new culture. Ask questions, make suggestions, and be involved.

If there is a restaurant in your area that specializes in the cuisine of the country you are studying, you might want to plan a field trip there with the language club. If you don't know what something is on the menu, ask the waitstaff. And don't be afraid to try new dishes and flavors.

or teach dances to share the various cultures. Or you might like to travel to a restaurant to sample traditional meals from that culture. You could go to a movie theatre to see an appropriate foreign film. Then you can talk about the movie over a meal or snacks at a restaurant. Perhaps you want to plan a trip abroad. This could be a trip your club plans to take or just an imaginary trip with a dream itinerary.

You may want to invite guest speakers to your meeting. Your advisor will help you identify guest speakers and presenters. Dancing groups, musicians, artists, or foreign exchange students from colleges or other high schools all make excellent guests. What would you like to hear about the culture and language? Knowing the answer to this question will help you choose an interesting speaker.

Language Club Activities

The foreign language club at Simms High School in Simms, Montana, holds an annual cultural night featuring an authentic dinner and a foreign movie. They also hold an annual crêpe and sopaipilla sale to help raise funds for a foreign trip.

Crêpes are a French creation resembling light, paper-thin pancakes. Dessert crêpes are often spread with a jam, fruit, or chocolate mixture, and served rolled or folded, while main course crêpes may be filled with meat, cheese, or vegetable mixtures.

Native to Mexican-American cuisine, the sopaipilla (which takes its name from the Spanish word for honey cake), is a crisp, puffy, deep-fried pastry resembling an air-filled pillow. Dessert sopaipillas are often served with honey or syrup flavored with anise or cinnamon. Main dish sopaipillas contain savory mixtures of meat, cheese, or vegetables.

Each year Gunn High School in Palo Alto, California, holds a weeklong International Festival. The festival was started years ago to help students become more aware of and appreciate other cultures. Through entertainment, ethnic foods, performances, special speakers, and even a parade, the entire school and community participate in this event.

The annual event began with students having the option to buy lunch featuring foods from other countries, rather than the typical school lunch. The students also watched a folk dance one day, enjoyed a flag parade another day, and cheered on their classmates during other student performances. The parade of flags showed students what each country's flag looked like. Students also dressed in costumes representing other countries. The event eventually grew into a weeklong International Festival.

To raise money from the event, World Language Club members sold tickets to nightly foreign movies, and they sold food—both for lunch and as snacks at the movies.

Will it cost anything to have this person or group visit your club?

Another activity you can plan for your club is a community service project. Perhaps you could host an international night for a senior center. Or the club could throw a party for a younger group of children using the theme of your club's language and culture. Service to your community may be simply picking up trash along a street, or collecting cans to recycle.

Whether you are interested in traveling abroad or hosting a foreign exchange student, there is a youth exchange/host program that will suit your needs.

4

Foreign Exchange Opportunities

Many students each year embark on a trip to a foreign country. For each of them, the first time they make such a long trip, they are a bit nervous, scared, and worried. Most experience some amount of homesickness. But that doesn't stop them from taking the opportunity to do something different.

You might climb the Swiss Alps, or swim in the Baltic Sea. Maybe you would ride the Camargue horses along the Rhône Delta in southern France. Standing on the top of Hadrian's Wall on a foggy morning in England transports you back to the days of Roman occupation of the island. If you love shopping, you might be able to visit one of Germany's largest department stores, the KaDeWe in Berlin, or visit the open air markets in various small towns across Europe.

Just as language clubs offer you an opportunity to expand your knowledge and understanding of a different culture, traveling to the country where that language is

Foreign Exchange Agencies

Here are some of the groups offering exchange programs.

Academic Year in America
River Plaza, 9 West Broad Street
Stamford, CT 06902-3788
ph: 1-800-322-HOST (4678)
www.academicyear.org

American Field Service (AFS)
71 West 23rd Street, 17th Floor, New York, NY 10010
ph: (800) AFS-INFO (in the U.S.) or (212) 807-8686
email: info.center@afs.org
www.afs.org

ASPECT Foundation Exchange Programs:
High School Year Abroad
Aspect International Language Academies
Shepherds West, Rockley Road, London, W14 0DA, UK
ph: +44 208 727 3550
email: enquiries@aspectworld.com
www.aspectworld.com

Academic Year in the USA Study Abroad
Organizational Headquarters
AYUSA International
2226 Bush Street, San Francisco, CA 94115
email: info@ayusa.org
www.ayusa.org/study_abroad

Council on International Educational Exchange (CIEE)
3 Copley Place 2nd Floor, Boston, MA 02116
ph: (617) 247-0350
email: info@councilexchanges.org
www.ciee.org

Cultural Homestay International (CHI)
CHI - Head Office (USA)
104 Butterfield Road, San Anselmo, CA 94960
ph: (415) 459-5397
email: chimain@msn.com
www.chinet.org

spoken shows you an entirely different way of life. Through your experiences in a different culture, you'll learn more about yourself, who you are and want to be. You'll learn more about your strengths and realize that you're stronger than you ever imagined.

Living overseas for any length of time lets you step outside of your own life to try on a different culture. You'll make friends with your host family and in the community. If you attend school while living abroad, you'll have the chance to meet other students your own age, too. Overseas travel changes your view on everything.

What is it like, traveling and living overseas? Each person will bring back something uniquely their own. You will be representing your country, your school, and your family to the host family, host school, and host country. But most important, you are representing yourself. The impression you leave behind will last a lifetime.

If your stay is only a few weeks, you'll typically spend a great deal of time sampling many different famous locations, foods, concerts, museums, festivals, carnivals, and other events. Shorter trips make for less time to relax and be bored, or to miss your family back home. Your stay will literally be packed from the time your plane touches down at the airport until you are welcomed back home by your family.

Longer homestays offer you a chance to truly experience life in the country of your choice. You'll have time to get to know your host family and really immerse yourself in the language and culture. If you choose to stay for a semester or year and attend school, you'll likely make many new friends (most exchange students are very popular in their host school).

You'll find out how to do laundry, what is on television,

Ismael Caballero, a sixteen-year-old Habitat for Humanity volunteer from Aleman Santamaria High School, volunteers in Cochabama, Bolivia, in 2001. For more information on Habitat for Humanity's volunteer opportunities abroad, contact <www.hfhi.org.>.

what it is like to go see a movie at the theatre. You may be able to watch some professional soccer or tennis matches or other sports. The many details of living in your home that you take for granted now will be seen from a new angle. You'll come to appreciate some of the everyday items we have that you can't find in other countries. (For example, in England it's difficult to find popcorn, except in bags of flavored popped corn.) You'll realize what the advantages of living in the other countries are over living in your hometown or your home country. You'll find out for yourself how people in other countries live and think, how they feel, and what they enjoy doing in their spare time.

Your host family will make sure you have good food to eat and a comfortable, private place to stay. They will encourage you to become a member of the family for at least the time that you stay with them. Many host families stay in touch with their exchange students for life, creating a second "adopted" family for the student.

The agencies that match students with families make sure that everyone shares common interests in sports, music, food, etc. Although many of the exchange programs do not require foreign language study, the more you've studied the easier it will be for you to understand conversations around you. Just by using your foreign language skills you'll become better at speaking, listening, and reading the language.

Most but not all of the exchange programs require you to be in high school to travel, especially for a semester or school year. Don't be upset if you aren't old enough now to go. Keep the exchange in mind as you study your foreign language and participate in your club's activities. You will be old enough before you know it. In the meantime, you can check out the language camps where you can go at any age. When you are old enough to go, your involvement with the language club will make it even easier for you to be considered for scholarships.

FOREIGN EXCHANGE AGENCIES

The U.S. Department of State has arranged for youth exchange programs that are funded by the Bureau of Educational and Cultural Affairs. These programs are run by foreign exchange agencies. Some of these programs encourage students from other countries to visit the United States. Others are looking for American students to travel abroad.

Once you've decided where you want to study abroad, the next step is to find the right program and funding. Scholarships are available from many sources, including the Rotary and Kiwanis Clubs.

Most exchanges to France, England, Italy, Germany, and other European countries are handled by a few of the foreign exchange agencies, though there are many agencies you can contact for information. (Be sure you and your parents are comfortable with an agency before spending any money).

The American Field Service (AFS)
<www.afs.org>

The American Field Service is one of the agencies that runs youth exchange programs funded by the Bureau of Education and Cultural Affairs. Their programs are created for students who are fifteen to eighteen years old. You will live with a host family in a community, and attend school for a semester, summer, or an entire year. The AFS offers exchanges to many countries, including France, Germany, England, and Australia.

Interamerican University Studies Institute (IUSI)
<www.iusi.org>

Interamerican University Studies Institute specializes in travel to Latin America and offers several high school programs for students who wish to study in Spanish-speaking countries. In 2004 they offered a trip to Costa Rica. Students explored the cultural and natural wonders of the country while improving their Spanish. Another trip is the "Arts in Mexico" summer Spanish tour, which blends Spanish language instruction with workshops on the culture and history of Mexico.

Adventures in Real Communication (ARC)
<www.arcyp.com>

Adventures in Real Communication is another agency that offers a variety of trips. Through them, you can visit France, Germany, Spain, Mexico, Costa Rica, Ecuador, Brazil, Japan, Russia, Australia, or Ireland for a period of weeks to an entire school year. You may travel as an individual adventurer or as part of a school group. They have a variety of programs to choose from.

Cultural Homestay International (CHI)
<www.chinet.org>

A non-profit organization that has been around for more than twenty years, Cultural Homestay International's emphasis is the education of the participating student, the host family, and the local community and school. More than 7,000 students visit at least ten different countries each year. They also offer summer programs to Spain.

Exchanges to Eastern Europe, Russia, and Central Asia

If you're interested in exchanging to Eastern Europe, Russia, or Central Asia, check out the following agencies:

Abroad in Russia
779 E. Merritt Island Cswy. #763, Merritt Island, FL 32952
ph: 1-866-889-9880
email: study@AbroadInRussia.com
www.AbroadInRussia.com

You must be at least sixteen years old and willing to travel to Russia.

American Councils for International Education: ACTR/ACCELS
1776 Massachusetts Ave. NW, Suite 700
Washington, D.C. 20036
ph: (202) 833-7522
email: harhdman@actr.org
www.actr.org

Arranges travel to Armenia, Kazakhstan, Russia, Turkmenistan, Ukraine, and Uzbekistan. Students with group leaders spend three to four weeks at one of the partner schools.

Colleges Abroad
3501-B N. Ponce De Leon Blvd., #353, St. Augustine, FL 32084
ph: (904) 827-0211
email: info@CollegesAbroad.com
www.collegesabroad.com

Students at least sixteen years old can travel to Russia for a summer, a semester, or a year-long program.

Council on International Educational Exchange
International Volunteer Projects
205 E. 42nd Street
New York, NY 10017
ph: 1-888-Council
email: info@ciee.org
www.ciee.org

For high school seniors wanting to volunteer overseas. You can work in Estonia, Lithuania, Russia, or the Ukraine for a two- to four- week community service project. You must be at least eighteen years old, and the trip price includes your room and board.

The Council on International Educational Exchange (CIEE)
<www.ciee.org>

The Council on International Educational Exchange offers many ways for students, parents, and teachers to travel abroad or host a foreign exchange student. If you want to improve your Spanish or Portuguese, you may want to travel to Brazil or Spain for a semester or an entire school year. You must be fifteen to eighteen years old and have finished two years of high school Spanish in order to go to Spain. If you'd rather go to France, you can go for a semester or school year if you have finished three years of high school French.

CIEE also combines language study with service projects in Costa Rica and Ecuador. You don't even need to know how to speak Spanish to go and build houses for Habitat for Humanity or work in an elementary school. If you just want to brush up on your French, you can travel for a month to France or Quebec City, Canada, for fun and language lessons.

ASPECT Foundation Exchange Programs: High School Year Abroad
<www.aspectworld.com>

For the ASPECT Foundation Exchange Program you need to be fifteen to eighteen years old to travel overseas and live with a host family while attending a local high school for a semester or a year. Through the ASPECT Program you can visit England, France, Germany, Ireland, or Uruguay. They offer courses you can take in the country where your target language is spoken. This approach helps you learn the language faster and easier than by studying it in a classroom in America.

The Academic Year in the USA Study Abroad (AYUSA)
<www.ayusa.org>

This program provides a way for high school students to live and study for a semester, school year, or summer overseas. This non-profit agency is another of the agencies offering government sponsored exchanges. You can do a summer exchange to Brazil, Ecuador, France, Japan, or Spain, or spend a semester or year of school in Australia, Brazil, Ecuador, England, Finland, Germany, France, Hungary, Japan, Netherlands, New Zealand, Norway, South Africa, Spain, or Sweden.

AYUSA also offers the Academic Year or Semester in the U.S. Program for students who want to spend time in America and improve their English language skills.

SCHOLARSHIPS

In addition to the many exchange agencies ready to make your foreign exchange a reality, you can also apply for a scholarship to help you afford the trip. Most do not require membership in a particular organization.

One of the first organizations to offer foreign exchange programs was Rotary International. They have provided opportunities for students and host families around the world since 1927, and from the United States since 1958. They offer long-term exchanges, which last for a school year, or short-term exchanges that include homestays, tours, and camps. Homestays usually mean living with a host family for a few weeks, while your host "brother" or "sister" comes to live with your family. Tours visit several countries with a group of teens from across America, or you might tour a country with a group of teens from around the world. Rotary offers several types of youth camps, including some where students from several countries are mixed

One way to travel abroad is to put your language skills to the test. These finalists in the National German Testing and Awards Program for High School Students were awarded a three-week study trip to Germany that includes a homestay experience. For more information on the program, contact <www.aatg.org>.

together to learn about leadership and discuss international problems. To apply, you need to be fifteen to nineteen years old, have above average grades, be able to express yourself easily, and show that you have leadership skills.

Ideally, Rotary International is looking for people who can be wonderful cultural ambassadors to the host countries. In exchange, you don't pay any agency fee for arranging the exchange. The host family pays for your room and board, and the host Rotary Club pays for any tuition expenses you may have at your new school. On longer visits, you may even qualify for a monthly allowance. Your costs include airfare, insurance, passports and visas, emergency funds, and any spending money you may want to take. To apply for this opportunity, contact

Because it is one of the most culturally diverse societies in the world, the United States is one of the most popular destinations for students choosing to travel abroad.

your local Rotary Club or visit their international Web site to locate a Rotary Club near you.

In 1983 the German and U.S. Congresses formed the Congress-Bundestag Youth Exchange Program (CBYX). Each year two hundred eighty American high school students are awarded scholarships to help America's youth gain an appreciation for current affairs, as well as German social, political, and economic lifestyles. The scholarship enables you to live and go to school in Germany for one year. You'll go to school and play a part in community life, culture, and recreation while you learn about the culture and country. Perhaps most important of all, you'll learn more about yourself. You do not need to be proficient in German to apply, but you do need to be flexible, curious, mature, and want to share who you are while learning

The Experiment in International Living

The Experiment in International Living offers dynamic summer programs for high school students in Europe, the Americas, Africa, Oceania, and Asia. For three to five weeks, program participants, who come from all over the world, visit another country where they are immersed in the daily life of another culture through a homestay experience, community service, language training, and activities related to ecology, arts, travel, and peace and conflict studies. Through experience-based learning, students build leadership and communication skills, increase their self-confidence, and enhance global awareness. Program participants develop a profound understanding of a different culture, language, and worldview, as well as the capacity to see their own lives and country in a much broader perspective.

In 2003, 980 students participated in the Experiment in International Living, traveling to 26 countries worldwide. Participants came from 42 U.S. states and 22 countries around the world, including Argentina, Belgium, Bermuda, Brazil, Canada, Costa Rica, Czech Republic, France, Guam, Hungary, Indonesia, Israel, Italy, Japan, Kenya, Korea, Mexico, Poland, South Africa, Turkey, Uganda, The United Arab Emirates, and the United Kingdom.

The Experiment in International Living is sponsored by World Learning, which also offers college study abroad programs in forty countries through its School for International Training.

For more information, contact:

> The Experiment in International Learning
> Kipling Road, P.O. Box 676
> Brattleboro, VT USA 05302-0676
> **ph:** (802) 257-775
> **toll free within the U.S.:** (800) 345-2929
> **fax:** 802-258-3428
> **email:** eil@worldlearning.org
> **www.usexperiment.org**

When traveling abroad, it is important to remain flexible and keep an open mind about trying new things. Just experiencing daily life can be a challenge when you are new to the language, traditions, and ways of a country.

about others. To apply, you must be a U.S. legal resident, have a grade point average of 3.0 or higher (on a 4.0 scale), and be fifteen to eighteen years old as of July 1st of the year in which you want to travel. Applications are due in mid-December and are available at the AYUSA Web site.

Another study abroad scholarship available at the AYUSA Web site is the Youth Leadership Scholarship, which is awarded to people based on availability, academic merit (i.e., your grades), and financial need. This scholarship is geared toward students who have a strong interest in service to the community, and who show how much they want to study abroad by trying on their own to raise the funds to travel. Deadlines for this application are January 1st and September 1st.

A Japan Youth Scholarship is provided through the

generosity of the United States Japan Foundation, which covers the cost for a full school-year long trip to live and study in Japan. You'll live with a Japanese host family and participate in community projects. Selection is based on merit, cultural interest, and evidence of your commitment to helping forge future U.S.-Japan relations. Deadline for this application is March 1st, and it is available through AYUSA.

The Council on International Educational Exchange (CIEE) offers several partial scholarships for their High School Semester or Year Abroad programs. You must write two short essays and get a letter from your parent or guardian, in addition to a teacher recommendation. Complete details and the application are available at the CIEE Web site.

If you happen to be a member of the Kiwanis Club's Key Club, you can apply for a scholarship to travel abroad. The AYUSA has partnered with the Kiwanis International Foundation to provide partial scholarships to study in twenty different countries. You must be a member of the Key Club to apply for one of these scholarships based on academic merit, cocurricular involvement, and financial need. Deadlines are January 1st and September 1st. The application is available through the AYUSA Web site.

HOSTING A FOREIGN EXCHANGE STUDENT

Many students don't want to travel abroad, but would like to have the fun of getting to know someone from another country. Perhaps your family could become a host family.

Host families volunteer to house and feed an international student for a period of weeks to months, sometimes even a year, to share their way of life with someone from a different country, and to learn about that other culture from an insider's view. A host family must be able to give the traveling student a safe, comfortable, and loving home during their stay. Hosting a foreign exchange student is a fun way to make a new, lifelong friend. You will have the chance to make your own foreign language skills stronger by talking with your exchange student.

Foreign Language Camps

These organizations offer intensive language training.

Concordia Language Villages
8659 Thorsonveien NE, Bemidji, MN 56601
ph: (800) 450-2214 or (218) 586-8600
www.cord.edu/dept/clv

International Camp in Canada
Ekocamp International
4433 Rive, ValoMorin, Quebec, J0T 2R0, Canada
ph: (819) 322-7051 or toll free in U.S. and Canada:
(888) 643-7012
email: info@ekocamp.com
http://ekocamp.com

Millersville University
Director, Summer Language Camps
Department of Foreign Languages
Millersville University, Millersville, PA 17551
ph: (717) 872-3526
email: camps@millersville.edu
www.muweb.millersville.edu/~forlang/hs-programs.html

Beloit Center for Language Studies
Patricia Zody, Ph.D., Director
Center for Language Studies
Beloit College
700 College Street, Beloit, WI 53511-5595
ph: (800) 356-0751 or (608) 363-2277
email: cls@beloit.edu
www.beloit.edu/~cls

No matter where you live—a big city, a small town, a chicken farm, or a condo overlooking the beach—if you have the room and the desire to share your lifestyle and viewpoint with someone else, and to make a good friend along the way, then you are eligible to become a host family.

The first step is to apply with a foreign exchange agency. The application gives information to the foreign student about what to expect when they arrive in your country. You and your family may be interviewed by the agency to ensure that the needs of the student are met, and to give you a chance to ask questions and prepare for your new visitor.

From your point of view, you'll need to consider if you want to have a short-term "sister" or "brother" come live with you. You'll be sharing the bathroom (most likely), the family room, including the television, games, etc., and your family with this person. Usually the students selected to be exchange students are polite, well-mannered individuals. Often, the foreign exchange student is popular at school merely because they are from another country. If you're willing to share, then you're ready for a wonderful opportunity.

If you and your family are interested in learning more about becoming a host family, contact any of the foreign exchange agencies for more information.

FOREIGN LANGUAGE CAMPS

If you can't travel abroad or welcome a foreign exchange student into your home, maybe you can attend a foreign language camp.

The Concordia Language Villages in Bemidji, Minnesota, offer separate camps in languages as varied as Chinese,

Danish, English, Finnish, French, German, Italian, Japanese, Korean, Norwegian, Russian, Spanish, and Swedish. Length of stay ranges from one weekend to a week or more.

The International Camp in Canada, called Ekocamp International, offers camps for students ten to sixteen and sixteen to twenty years old, learning French or English. Ekocamp provides weekly language training (fifteen hours); qualified, experienced teachers; books and educational materials (which are included in the camp cost); and achievement diplomas to each participant. Typical activities include French immersion, swimming, water skiing, river canoeing with overnight camping, horseback riding, wilderness survival, field trips to Montreal or Quebec City, and more.

Millersville University provides Foreign Language Camps in French, German, and Spanish each year. In 2004 they offered a Russian Heritage Camp for the first time, open to fifteen- to eighteen-year-olds who have a Russian ethnic background. The other language camps are taught by high school teachers on the campus. Camp participants must have had two years of language and be at least fifteen years old, though some exceptions have been made for students who have studied abroad or grown up with the language.

If you are studying or would like to study Arabic, Chinese, Czech, Hungarian, Japanese, Portuguese, Russian, or Spanish, you can try the Beloit Center for Language Studies. This is an intensive summer language program held at their Wisconsin campus for four-and-a-half or nine-week sessions. This is an immersion program, but you do not need to have taken the language to go to the beginning program camps.

Whether you decide to host an exchange student in your home, study abroad yourself, or attend a foreign language camp, the experience will enhance your understanding of another culture and leave you with memories that will last a lifetime.

Planning and executing a successful fundraiser requires leadership and teamwork from the club members, but it can also be a lot of fun.

5

Paying Your Way

Now that you know what activities you want to do in your club, you might need to raise money to pay for them. Raising money may be as simple as collecting dues or donations from each member, or you might need to earn money to pay your way.

Choose a club fundraiser that is fun as well as profitable. If you and the club members are all having fun with the fundraising activity, the members will stick with it and probably collect more money.

First, figure out how much money you need to raise. Some costs to consider include food (snacks at meetings or meals while traveling), travel expenses (gas money or bus rental), admissions, and a miscellaneous category for unexpected expenses. Try to raise only enough money to meet your goals—you don't need a lot left over.

To track how much you've spent versus how much you've earned, use a spreadsheet program (like Excel or Lotus), or use a simple balance sheet listing debits and credits. The type of fundraiser you choose will also help you decide when you'll collect money. For example, if you decide to sell a product, your customers might have to pay for items as they order them, or pay for them when you deliver the items.

The club should decide who will lead the fundraising project. Choose someone who is responsible, friendly, and organized to lead this important task. Fundraising committees are often most effective. The committee chair will call the meetings and map the group's progress, making sure the club is working toward their goal.

Be smart about how and where you sell products. Sell to people you know first. Ask your parents and grandparents to ask their friends and business associates. E-mail messages and phone calls are good ways to spread the word about your fundraising effort without walking on unknown streets. If you do end up selling door-to-door, never sell alone or after dark. Also, never enter a stranger's house or carry a lot of money.

Now that you know how much you need to raise, and who is leading the effort, it's time to choose how you'll raise the money.

Spreading the Word

To let other students and possibly the community at large know about your club's fundraising efforts, try these ideas:

- Post announcements and flyers
- Send out newsletters
- Send press releases to the local papers
- Tell the PTA and other parent groups

Bake sales and cookie sales are one way to raise funds for your language club. You might want to try making cookies that are traditional to a certain region or culture, such as Scottish shortbread or Greek wedding cookies.

FUNDRAISING IDEAS

Here are some ways your club can finance your fun activities:

Special Dinner. Language clubs across the country host a dinner that features food from a foreign country, as well as other related activities. Some schools combine all the language club dinners into one multicultural event.

Bake sale. Cookies, cakes, pies, brownies, blueberry muffins. Bake up some American as well as ethnic goodies, and rake in the dough.

Personalized cookies. You might want to take the bake sale concept a step further by making holiday cookies in the shape of eggs, hearts, or four-leaf clovers, for example, (depending on which holiday is approaching). Then take orders to personalize the cookies with messages. Decorator icing in a tube is easy to write with on the cookies. If the customer wants the cookies delivered, charge a bit more for the convenience.

Pizza sale. Simply take orders for a few types of pizza (pepperoni, veggie, cheese) and collect the money for them. Then on a specific Saturday, the club puts the pizzas together. The customers show up to pick up their pizzas at a designated time and place. Remember to include pizza boxes in your expenses.

Flower and plant sale. Late winter is a great time to take orders for plants and bulbs. Check with a local nursery or the local garden club to see if they can help you with cost and delivery. Take orders for the plants, collecting the money from customers when the orders are placed. Set up a specific time and place for customers to pick up their plants.

Breakfast with Santa. One or more language clubs can join forces to host a Christmas breakfast, complete with Santa. You could set up booth space for local boutiques and shops to rent to sell their gift items. Parents then can shop while the children eat an ethnic breakfast. Each language club might even have someone dress up like a Christmas Eve visitor from that country.

Raffle a Getaway Trip. Ask a parent or your advisor to arrange for donations or at-cost items from businesses. A popular raffle item might be an airplane ticket to a nearby city for a weekend getaway, complete with a limo or carriage ride, gourmet dinner, and a night or two at a luxury hotel. To busy parents and others, this is a wonderful idea, making for a very popular raffle.

Skating party. Ask your local skating rink (ice, roller or inline skate) if you can hold a skating party. Have your club sell tickets that include skates, admission, and a donation to the club. You might ask the rink owner if you can set up a refreshment stand to make some more money for your club.

Chuck a Puck. Some clubs have made a lot of money with this idea. Essentially, you sell rubber ice hockey pucks at the ice rink. Then between periods, everyone who bought a puck throws them onto the ice, aiming for center ice. The closest puck to center ice wins half the money. You only need to buy the pucks, make up posters, set up tables for puck sales, and have a bunch of club members ready to gather up the pucks.

Halloween Costume Dinner Dance. You can hold this at your school or a local restaurant. Sell tickets that cover the cost of the dinner and a band or D.J. for the evening. You may want to hold a costume contest with prizes for the funniest or scariest costume. Be sure to sell dance-only tickets as well.

If you don't want to host an event, you can also choose from a wide range of fundraiser items to sell. You might want to sell engraved bricks to create a new sidewalk and raise some money for your school. Or sell teddy bears wearing T-shirts with your school logo or another saying printed on it. Other items include candles, candy, hats, shirts, first aid kits, colorful trash bags, and more.

SPONSORS

Many people and businesses are willing to donate money or items to a group to help them raise money. For example, if you wanted to raffle off a new bike, the local bike store might give you the bike to raffle, or sell it to you at cost (the store owner's price) rather than at retail (the customer's usual price).

You need to make a plan with your fellow club members and your advisor. Make a list of possible sponsors: family, friends, parents' friends, stores, etc. Before you ask these folks to help you, work out in writing what you want to say to them. Practice saying what you've written, and you will sound and feel more confident when asking potential sponsors for a donation.

An example of what you might say could be: "Hello. The French Club at Lakeview Middle School is raising money for a trip to Montreal. Could you help us with a donation?"

Keep in mind that you should look the potential sponsor in the eyes as you talk, and remember to smile. Dress neatly, wear clean clothes, comb your hair, and be friendly. Adults like students who dress neatly and are polite, and you're more likely to get a donation that way.

Your parents have probably told you that when someone gives you something you should say thank you. This is even more important when someone donates money or items to your club. Sponsors enjoy helping students reach their goals, and most proudly display the thank-you letters the groups send. Sponsors are more open to giving your club future donations if you thank them.

Types of Fundraisers

You can choose from two basic kinds of fundraisers: direct sales and order taking.

Direct sales is simply when a group has an item in stock and sells the item directly to the customer. The benefit is that you only have to meet each customer once—when you sell the item. This is also a faster way of making money, since you don't have to take orders, place the order, receive the order, then deliver it. However, it's very easy to have too much stock and not enough customers, leaving someone's garage stacked up with boxes of chocolate bars, stuffed bears, or baseball caps.

Order taking is what you've probably done before for school fundraisers. You show potential customers a catalog of items that they can choose from. You take the orders, place an order with the supplier, receive the items and sort them out, then deliver them to the customer. While this takes longer, you also don't have the risk of having too many items. But you might have customers change their mind about paying for the items between the time they order them and when you deliver them.

Your club will need to decide which form works best for you.

Thank-you letters and certificates of appreciation can easily be created and signed by all the club members or just the fundraising committee. Or you can make something more creative—a decorated candle, a candy jar full of ethnic goodies, or a signed photo of the group. Consider how your group can make the thank-you represent what you are doing—having fun while exploring and understanding another culture.

Glossary

advisor–a person who gives advice to another person or group.

direct sales–a method of fundraising in which an item in stock is sold directly to a customer.

donator–a person or business who gives or presents something.

fundraiser–an event held to raise money.

homestay–a period during which a visitor in a foreign country lives with a local family.

order taking–a method of fundraising in which customers select a product from a catalog and receive the item at a later date.

passport–a formal document issued by an authorized official of a country to one of its citizens for the purpose of exit from and reentry into the country.

scholarship–money given to a student to pay for class tuition and expenses.

sponsor–a person or business who donates money or items to a group or club, usually in exchange for recognition by the club.

visa–an endorsement made on a passport showing that it is valid and that the bearer may proceed.

Internet Resources

http://exchanges.state.gov/education/citizens/students/programlist.htm
> List of exchange programs endorsed by the U.S. State Department Youth Exchange Programs.

www.aatsp.org
> Web site of the American Association of Teachers of Spanish and Portuguese.

www.aatseel.org
> Web site of the American Association of Teachers of Slavic and Eastern European Languages.

www.ciee.org
> The Council on International Educational Exchange (CIEE) provides information for individuals interested in working or studying abroad as well as host families and employers.

www.csun.edu/~hcedu013/karin.html
> A useful online list of high school foreign exchange programs.

www.rotary.org
> The Web site of Rotary International, which sponsors students on foreign exchange programs.

www.exchanges.state.gov
> The Bureau of Educational and Cultural Affairs at the U.S. Department of State provides updated travel, visa, and passport information, as well as service information and emergency warnings for Americans traveling or living abroad.

Further Reading

Allen, Caron, Linda Duke, and Natsumi Watanabe. *A Homestay in Japan: "Nihon to No Deai"*. Berkeley, California: Stone Bridge Press, 1992.

Gensheimer, Cynthia F. *Raising Funds for Your Child's School: Over Sixty Great Ideas for Parents and Teachers*. New York: Walker & Company, 1993.

Hansel, Bettina G. *Exchange Student Survival Kit*. Yarmouth, Maine: Intercultural Press, Inc., 1993.

Joachim, Jean. *Beyond the Bake Sale: The Ultimate School Fund-Raising Book*. New York: St. Martin's Press, 2003.

King, Nancy, and Ken Huff. *Host Family Survival Kit: A Guide for American Host Families*. Yarmouth, Maine: Intercultural Press, 1997.

Libby, Megan McNeill. *Postcards from France*. New York: Harper Collins, 1998.

Stier, William F. *Fund-Raising for Sport and Recreation*. Champaign, Illinois: Human Kinetics Publishers, 1995.

Index

PICTURE CREDITS

ABOUT THE AUTHOR

Betty Bolté is a freelance writer and editor. She has written several books, a monthly newspaper column, and more than fifty general interest articles. Bolté graduated from Indiana University in 1995 with a degree in English and a minor in Anthropology. She lives on a horse farm in Taft, Tennessee, with her husband, two teenagers, and her father.

SERIES CONSULTANT

Series Consultant Sharon L. Ransom is Chief Officer of the Office of Standards-Based Instruction for Chicago Public Schools and Lecturer at the University of Illinois at Chicago. She is the founding director of the Achieving High Standards Project: a Standards-Based Comprehensive School Reform project at the University of Illinois at Chicago, and she is the former director of the Partnership READ Project: a Standards Based Change Process. Her work has included school reform issues that center on literacy instruction, as well as developing standards-based curriculum and assessments, improving school leadership, and promoting school, parent, and community partnerships. In 1999, she received the Martin Luther King Outstanding Educator's Award.